SPUNKY'S DIARY

Janette Oke

SPUNKY'S DIARY

Janette Oke

Illustrated by
Brenda Mann

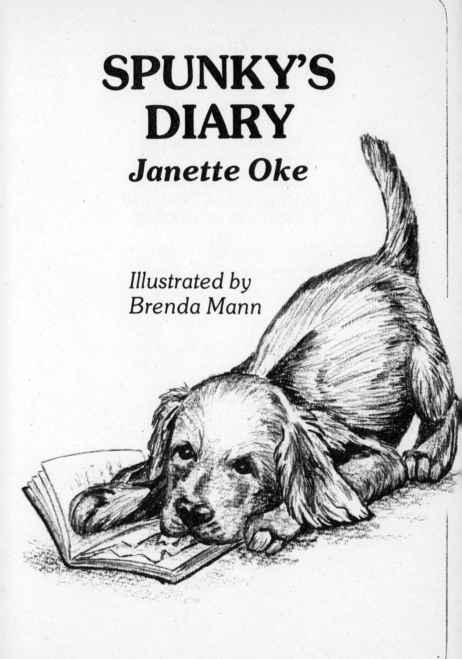

Other Janette Oke
Children's Books in this Series:

NEW KID IN TOWN
THE PRODIGAL CAT
DUCKTAILS
THE IMPATIENT TURTLE
A COTE OF MANY COLORS
PRAIRIE DOG TOWN
MAURY HAD A LITTLE LAMB
TROUBLE IN A FUR COAT
THIS LITTLE PIG
PORDY'S PRICKLY PROBLEM
WHO'S NEW AT THE ZOO

Copyright © 1982
Bethel Publishing Company
All Rights Reserved

Published by
Bethel Publishing Company
1819 South Main Street
Elkhart, Indiana 46516

Cover Illustration by
Brenda Mann

Printed in the United States of America

ISBN 0-934998-55-8

Dedicated with love
to the young - and
to those who remember being so.

Table of Contents

Chapter 1

My Family

I suppose, like most humans, you think it a bit strange for a dog to have a diary.

Susan Smith had one. John Boy Walton had one. Anne Frank had one—and I saw no reason whatever why I shouldn't be allowed the pleasure of one too.

I will admit that Mama reacted questioningly when I told her of my intention. At first she looked shocked, as though I had lost all dog-sense; then she smiled to herself, amused at her rather far-out pup. I didn't let it discourage me though. Once I had made up my mind about a matter, I stuck with it like a burr-in-a-dog's-coat, or however the saying goes. Anyway, I'm glad that I did. I've had a lot of enjoyment from my diary over the years, and especially now that I'm older and not as active as I used to be. My only regret is that I didn't keep it up more faithfully.

I like to flip through the pages reminiscing a bit. Sometimes it even brings a lump to my throat. Oh, well, guess maybe being senile and sentimental sort of go hand in hand.

I suppose that I should share with you a little of my family background. We lived in an "average" section of the town, with an "average" family to care for. When I say "average," I mean just that. Would you believe that their name was "Smith." There was Mr. Thomas Smith whom we referred to as "He" and Mrs. Margaret Smith, known as "She." Then there was Tom Smith Jr. (we just called him "Jr.") and Susan Smith, our favorite, known to us all as "Susie."

My mother was rather cosmopolitan, being of mixed blood, though she never did let us forget that our great, great grandfather on her mother's side had royal blood, being a fully-registered Cocker Spaniel. Mama carried herself with great dignity and expected no less of her offspring.

There were five of us in the litter. The oldest was named Blackie by the Smith children. Mama didn't approve much of the unimaginative and inappropriate names given to us by the Smiths and named us herself, with names that she considered more in keeping with our heritage. Blackie was to Mama, and thus to the rest of us also, Bruno II, named after our father. Bruno II was the biggest of the litter and was inclined to throw his weight around. He had a quick temper too, and I soon learned that we got along just fine as long as I stayed in my place, but it was so easy to forget that, and I have scars to prove it.

Number Two was my sister Treena; the Smiths called her Brownie. Treena was okay as sisters go, but she could be a bit bossy at times. However, if you could overlook her I-told-you-so attitude and her bossiness, she could also be motherly and generous, though goodness knows how many times I wished that she wouldn't fuss so.

I was next in line, right in the middle of the litter. I think that Mama often wondered what would ever become of me. I can recall her saying, with a deep sigh, "I honestly don't know what to do with you,"

but after she said it, she would pull me close and lick my face clean and kiss the nose that was so often in someone else's business. The Smiths called me Spot because of the small white patch on my forehead, but Mama named me Spunky.

Next was another sister, Lucky to the Smiths. Mama named her Little Majesty. She was the one who showed her royal blood line the most. She was so prim and proper about everything, especially when Mama was watching. Get her in the right mood though and she could be more fun than a barrel of donkeys or however that saying goes. She and I had loads of fun together and were the ones Mama would most often have to scold to settle down at night. We loved to lie close together whispering jokes and secrets to one another, and though she often howled until her silky sides shook, I knew that she never laughed at me, only with me.

The baby and the smallest of the litter was named Minx, by Mama that is, and here was a real sore spot with her. The Smiths couldn't seem to settle on a name and were always alternating Tiny and Runt or Peewee. Now, that "Runt" really got under Mama's skin. I could fairly feel her bristle everytime she heard them use it. She felt that it was a real insult to a fine family. There were times when the Smiths were showing off the litter that I saw Mama deliberately move a leg over Minx, hoping that they would forget that he was there. They never did of course, for Minx seemed to be a favorite. Girls would squeal, "Oh isn't she darling," and again Mama would stiffen. It seems that humans have the idea that if you're small, you're female.

Minx was an easy-going, happy-go-lucky little guy. Guess he knew that he'd never make out too well in a fight so he decided to clown his way through life instead. It worked for him too. Everybody loved him.

Oh yes—Mama! The Smiths called her Lady but Mama preferred to use her **real** name. I was glad that I could call her Mama instead, for everytime that I tried her name I stumbled over it. It was a real mouthful but Mama believed that it carried some of the dignity due to one with some royal blood. After all she was sort of a Princess, wasn't she? Her Mama too had been very proud of her bloodline and had given all of her children impressive names accordingly. My Mama's name was Mandelle Zephery, said very softly and with a great deal of feeling. Mandelle Zeph-ery.

Besides our family and the Smiths, the only other occupant of the house was Samantha, an orange-striped tabby cat of fair proportions. Mama said that when she was younger she had been sleek and well-built but with age she had sort of let herself go. Besides she was a bit too fond of rich milk to keep her figure trim. She and Mama had sort of a gentlelady's agreement; peaceful co-existence, Mama called it, though I never did know exactly what that meant. Anyway, things went quite smoothly. Samantha liked to put on airs, and often cast glances Mama's way in a rather disdainful manner. As for Mama, she just pretended that Samantha wasn't even there. Her very attitude said clearly, "Let her sit there and put-on-the-cat; she doesn't impress me one bit."

So that's the way that my life began. Warm and cared for. Mama loved each one of us, and the Smiths in their own human way seemed pleased with us too.

Chapter 2

My Diary

Susie Smith often chose one of us to take to her room for a short while in the evenings. It was while I was there one night that I got the idea of a diary. I had just chewed on the arm of one of Susie's favorite dolls and received a spank on the behind for it, so I had crawled off in the corner of her bed to sulk. Susie sat at her desk and as she wrote she talked to herself. She was writing in her diary. About that time her big brother came in.

"Watcha doin'?"

"Writin' in my diary."

"What for? Diaries are dumb!"

"They are not. Someday I can look back an' read all of the fun things I've done."

"That all you write? Fun things?"

"Course not. I put everything. Just like it happens."

"Still think it's dumb."

"It is not."

"Is too."

"Is not."

"Is too."

"Why don't you get out?"

"Cause I need someone to play Snakes an' Ladders with."

"Not me. I'm busy."

"Just bein' dumb."

Jr. went out and slammed the door; Susie started talking to herself again. I listened more carefully now. She was telling about her shopping trip with her mother and the new red shoes that they bought and the chocolate malt that she had talked her mother into buying, then dribbled on her best sweater.

I liked the idea of a diary. I decided right then and there that I'd have one too, so I started the very next morning.

June 6—(Mama said that's the day it is today.) Today I told Majesty my seekrit. She laughed.

June 7—I had a tug-of-war with Treena. I almost won.

June 8—This was not a nice day. I got a spank for wetting on the rug.

June 9—Today Bruno II tried to chase S'mantha. She slapped him and made him cry.

June 10—Today I drank from a dish. It had milk. "She" pushed my nose in. I licked it. It was good. "She" pushed it in again. I liked it. I pushed it in. My back part came up and tipped me over. I fell right in getting all my face wet. Treena scolded me for being so clumsy, but she cleaned me up.

June 11—Today I hurt. "He" stepped on my tail.

June 12—Today Minx and I found a slipper. We sure had fun. It looks kinda messy. Hope "He" doesn't find out who did it!

June 13—We got put outside several times today for "training." Don't know what that means but we sure had fun in the flower bed.

June 14—We went outside for "training" again. When we came back in Bruno II went to the corner and "She" yelled.

June 15—Outside again. I didn't like it. It was raining

and my paws got wet and cold. Mama had to clean and clean when we got back to our bed.

June 16—"She" says Little Majesty is "trained." She still looks alright to me.

June 17—We had some *other stuff* from a dish today. It was lumpy and you had to mess it around in your mouth before you could swallow it. It was funny stuff but Bruno II said that it was good so I ate it too.

June 18—Treena was really bossy today. Mama says that she is getting *that age*. Sure hope that she's not *that age* again tomorrow. I get tired of her fussing. I told her that I didn't need to 'bey her and she couldn't push me around and Majesty just giggled.

June 19—"She" feeds us from a dish a lot now. I like the milk but I'm not sure about the lumpy stuff. Treena says that you have to 'velope taste for it, whatever that means.

June 20—Today Bruno II decided to have some fun with Samantha when Mama wasn't looking. He sneaked up when Samantha was sleeping in the sun and jumped, bang, right on her middle. Samantha sure did look funny. She scolded and scolded Mama 'bout teaching her family some decent manners. Mama 'pologized and sent Bruno II to bed but I saw Mama sort of smile when Samantha walked away with her back still up.

June 21—A dull day today. Nothing happened that was 'citing.

June 22—We sure had 'citement today. I barked at the mailman when he wasn't looking. The mailman jumped, missed a step and fell down on the walk on his hands and knees. His mail spilled all over the walk; the wind was blowing his letters and all the Smiths ran and ran catching them until they were red-faced and funny. The mailman yelled, waved his hands, and shook his fists, and I hid under the porch until they all quieted down and went away. Mama was 'shamed of me.

June 23—Mama was still upset today. She says if we don't soon learn some manners we'll all be in trouble.

June 24—Today was a happy day. Susie Smith took us all to the backyard to play. We saw a butterfly. It looked like a flower that got turned loose. The sun was nice on our backs when we had our sleep. Mama was happy again too and played a game of "fight and wrestle" with us.

June 25—Little Majesty and I had a real fun time. We found a book on the floor and 'tended it was an *enemy* and dragged it and pulled it and growled at it and everything. It tore a lot, and then we chased pieces and jumped on them and shook them and scattered them. We sure fixed the *enemy*. Then Susie came home and yelled real loud, "My library book," and Majesty and I hid under the bed.

Chapter 3

Changes

Well that's the way that my diary was begun. I guess that at the time I just expected that life would always go on in the same fashion for all of us. I was very naive you see and knew nothing about the world out there. Mama didn't say much about it either, but then came a day that changed everything for all of us. I will never forget it.

The first thing that drew my attention was a change in Mama. I couldn't quite decide what it was, but I could feel that it was there.

Since we had been eating a lot of our meals from a dish, Mama was spending less and less time with us in our bed. She sometimes would even push us away, or get up and leave if we became too demanding. Susie said that she was "pushing us from the nest." We didn't even live in a nest! Anyway we were sort of getting used to being nudged away and made to spend more time on our own, so I knew that something had happened when Mama came in from outside and looked around anxiously. She then called us to our bed and

when we'd all been gathered in, she climbed in with us
and drew us all close, nosing and licking each one of us.
I was the last one to have a turn and I was sure that as I
looked at Mama her eyes were misty. By then most of
the others were already curled up, full and sleepy.

I wanted to ask Mama about it all but I just couldn't.
I wished with all of my heart that I could comfort her
some way and take the troubled look from her eyes. I
tugged at her ear playfully, thinking that maybe that
would distract her but she pulled me closer and said
softly, "Spunky, whatever will become of you?" and
the mist deepened, forming a tear that trickled across
her cheek. I licked it away and snuggled up against her
but I just couldn't go to sleep.

When Mama thought that we were all sleeping, she
gently licked each member of the litter again and then
quietly left the box. I heard her lapping water and then
she lay down under the kitchen table with a deep sigh. I
opened one eye and peeked out from our bed. Samantha, a bit pudgy but still arrogant, sat under the table
too, washing her already clean coat. Suddenly she quit
washing and looked across at Mama.

"I see the *sign* is up again."

"Yes," Mama sighed, "I saw it too."

Samantha sort of sneered.

"'Cute puppies to give away,'" she repeated carefully. "Do you suppose anyone will want them?"

"They always do," Mama responded evenly, refusing
to take the bait.

"Well, I certainly hope so," said Samantha, empha-
sizing each word. "It would be wonderful to have some
peace and quiet around here—and soon."

"Yes," said Mama. "It would be quiet."

"Well, it's your problem," purred Samantha. "I'm
certainly glad that it isn't mine. 'Cute puppies to give
away,'" she repeated with another sneer. "My word,
haven't you raised *enough* puppies for them to give
away. I don't know why you continue to allow it. Why

they had me cared for some time back.''

"Yes,'' said Mama, with a great deal of careless nonchalance. "I suppose puppies *are* easier to give away than kittens.''

Samantha's eyes narrowed and her back came up slightly. I was sure that I could see her working her claws but she said nothing. She cast a disdainful glance at Mama, then our box, another at Mama, and left the room.

Mama laid her head back on her paws. She had beaten Samantha in her own way, but I could tell that her heart was still heavy. I now knew why, but I still didn't understand what it was all about.

The next day things went pretty well as normal. We ate and slept and growled and tumbled. We chewed whatever we found and teased Samantha when Mama wasn't looking. Bruno II shouldered his way through us whenever we had something that he wanted. Treena scolded and nipped and bossed, then smothered and mothered and soothed. Little Majesty pranced with great dignity and then collapsed into a rolling ball of soft laughter over some silly act or words of mine. Minx clowned his way through the day adding fun to the lives of each of us, and I - I was just me, Spunky, enjoying life to the full.

That evening, Mama joined us in our bed again and after she carefully washed and caressed each one of us, she began in a careful voice.

"I trust that whatever happens in life, you will remember your bloodline and your training. You have reason to hold your head high and walk proud. You will be an asset to any family. Always remember that.''

"Remember too, that because you are *somebody* you have freedom to make *somebody* of others less fortunate than you. You don't need to *prove* yourselves. You will be free to think of others and to help them feel that they are worthwhile too. This is a mark of good breeding. Think of others—not self, for in so doing you will find happiness and true contentment."

"You will have new masters. Seek to bring to them devotion and happiness and add something special to their lives. This is fulfilling your station in life, for dogs, first class dogs, were intended to give man what he misses in his topsy-turvy world—love. That's our purpose, and we fulfill it so capably."

"There are simple manners too that I want you to remember. My mother taught them to me and I have tried to teach them to you. They are known as the Rules of Good Conduct. Remember them. They are of utmost importance to all obedient and loving dogs.

1. Seek always to love your master.

2. Be obedient, insofar as you can understand his orders.

3. Do not forsake your master's voice to follow after others.

4. Allow yourself to be handled and cuddled, and as much as possible, appear to enjoy it.

5. Respect other dogs' boundaries.

6. Be prepared to defend what belongs to your master.

7. Eat neatly—accepting what is provided for you.

8. Do not beg while your family is dining.

9. Avoid cats and other objectional creatures, but if they cannot be avoided, do your best to live in harmony.

10. Ask with your eyes before assuming new territory in the home."

It seemed an awful lot for a small pup to remember but I had watched Mama observing each one of those rules in her daily living, and I knew that seeing her live them would help me to remember them.

Mama licked us again.

"You'd best get some sleep now," she said, and because we were tired from a busy day we snuggled up against her without argument. Bruno II took up too much room and Treena had a heavy paw stretched across my middle. I wiggled free and cuddled close to

Little Majesty. Minx lay gently against my back. I took one last lick at Little Majesty, laid my head on her silky side and went to sleep.

Chapter 4

Majesty

People came. Little girls squealed and boys hauled us out of bed and stroked us and fondled us. We licked the faces of all of them and they pleaded with their Moms and Dads, "Can we have one, please, please?"

One family came in and cried out and handled and exclaimed, and we all tried to be friendly with them as we had been taught by Mama. Their girl giggled and talked with Susie Smith and laughed and said, "Oh they're so cute, I wish that I could have them all." When they left they took Little Majesty with them. I couldn't understand it and kept waiting and fussing all day wondering when they would bring her back, but when it was time to go to sleep she still hadn't come.

I crawled off to a corner of the box and whimpered. I missed her soft fur and the giggling over secrets. Mama came then. I pushed up close against her and asked her when Majesty would be coming home, but she shook her head and a tear fell down each cheek.

"She has a *new* home now," she said, "and a new master. She won't be coming back to us now. Not ever.''

I couldn't believe it. I didn't like being without Little Majesty. Who would laugh when I told a joke or rolled up in a nylon stocking? I wanted to cry, but Mama went on.

"You will all have new homes, Son. Remember well your up-bringing and make your Mama proud. It will be lonely at first, but if you follow the Rules you will find happiness with your new master. I hope that you will all find kind and good humans to care for. Be brave, and be proud. Your Mama's proud of you.''

Chapter 5

Minx

June 29 — Today Minx left us. He looked so little as he was carried away. Mama wagged her tail at the people who came but her eyes pleaded with them to please, please leave her baby. They didn't seem to notice. The lady carried Minx to the car. The little boy was still too small to carry a dog properly, even a very small dog like Minx. The boy had insisted upon holding Minx though, and I couldn't help but realize that Minx must have been terribly uncomfortable. He had just finished his lunch and his little tummy was bulging, but the boy didn't seem to realize that. He hung Minx over his pudgy arm, hind legs hanging down awkwardly on one side and front legs drooping over the other. I hoped with all of my heart that Minx wouldn't bring up his lunch. He didn't. He even managed to get a lick at the little boy's face. The boy squealed with delight. I was proud of Minx.

They started off to their car. I saw Minx look back once, a puzzled, longing look on his face. I knew that he wanted to run back to Mama. She had been lying quietly under a lawn chair but she stood suddenly and took a couple of steps forward, and then, as though following the command of some inner voice, she held herself back, but I could hear the soft whimper that escaped her throat and I knew that she was hurting.

After the car had pulled away from the curb, Mama watched it until it turned a corner three blocks away and then she left. I knew that she wanted to be alone, so I didn't follow her.

I went back to Bruno II and Treena. We were all missing Majesty and Minx and our loneliness drove us to curl up together, forgetting all of our usual disagreements as to who was crowding whom, and nuzzling one another as we sought to go to sleep.

Mama came back later in the day and cleaned us up. She pulled us all close against her and licked us thoroughly. Our little pink tongues managed, in turn, an occasional lick of her face, and then we settled down against her to go to sleep.

I still felt lonely, just as I knew Mama did, but as long as I had her I knew that I'd never be really alone. The thought of ever being separated from Mama never even entered my mind, though I realized later that Mama had tried hard to prepare each one of us for that very thing. I snuggled up close to her and went to sleep with the comforting sound of her beating heart as my assurance.

Chapter 6

My New Family

June 30 — There have been a few other visitors to the Smith household—mostly children who had seen the sign and stopped to check out the puppies. They had left determined to talk their parents into allowing them to have a dog. Bruno II, Treena, and I have been handled and exclaimed over many times, it seems.

Bruno II has a tendency to get a bit upset with the carelessness of some of the children, and sometimes he lets it show. Last night Mama scolded him and reminded him of his duty to man. Bruno II stuck up for himself by saying that the boy had hurt him. Mama looked at him softly, imploring him to listen carefully and to try with all of his heart to remember to live by her words.

"Son, many times in life you may be hurt, not always through maliciousness, most often by carelessness, but whatever the circumstance, you must learn to never, never hurt back. Remember, you are a gentleman; you have a name to uphold, a heritage. Never become so small, so self-seeking that you try revenge or retaliation. Win your master's approval through devotion, Son, devotion and obedience. If you cannot win in that manner, then accept the fact that you are a loser, but lose with dignity, with your head held high. Never cower or crawl; but never become snappish or mean; just turn your back and walk away."

As I listened, I wondered if Bruno II would be able to honor my Mama's words. He said nothing, but I could see the determination still flickering in his eyes.

I had a difficult time getting to sleep without Majesty and Minx. Treena fussed at my tossing about. When I whined back to her about my sleep problem, she pushed me away from her and said, "Well for goodness sake then, count goats so the rest of us can have some peace."

July 1 — This morning some new people came. I watched as they handled first Bruno II and then Treena. It surprised me when the boy called out, "Hey, look at this one," and pulled me out from under the chair where I was silently observing the commotion.

I remembered Mama's instructions and tried to wiggle my stubby tail. I'm afraid that my whole body squirmed along with it. I licked the boy's face and he giggled with pleasure.

"I want this one, please, Mama, please," he begged.

A girl crossed over to look at me.

"He is cute, isn't he?"

"Please, Mama. This one, please," the boy continued to coax.

I paid no mind to the pleading but continued to lick his face and his hands whenever I could get a good lick in, and shook my small body in an effort to get my tail to wag.

When they started to the door I suddenly realized that the boy still hadn't put me down. He followed his mother to their car and the girl clamored along behind.

"Can I have a turn holding him please?"

"On the way home," the boy promised.

He opened the car door and climbed in, still holding
me. I barked a quick sharp little bark to remind him
that I was still there, but he just laughed some more
and the mother started the car.

I scampered quickly up on his shoulder where I could
see out of the window. Mama stood there, her feet
slightly apart, her eyes holding mine, and as the car
moved off I heard her soft whine. I knew then that it
was going to be with me as it had been with Little
Majesty and Minx and a hard lump came into my throat.
A wave of fear and loneliness washed over me, making
a shiver pass through my body. It had never occurred
to me in spite of Mama's warnings that I might be taken
from her. I had watched the others go, completely
oblivious to the fact that my turn might come as well.
Now I fully understood the sadness in Mama's eyes
each time that she watched one of her babies being
carried away. A little cry came struggling up from deep
within me and left my throat as a soft, sad whine. The
boy pulled me back into his arms.

"Ah, he's sad," said the girl.

The boy said nothing, but stroked my shiny coat and
nuzzled my face with his finger. I could tell that he liked
me and a little of the sadness began to seep away from
me. Eventually I dozed.

I awoke being passed from one pair of hands to another, for it was now the girl's turn to hold me. She
reached for me eagerly but gently, and soon I was in
her lap being fondled and spoken to softly.

"You are just a little sweetie," she crooned. "You
are gonna be so much fun."

I snuggled up against the warmth of her and again
went to sleep.

The next time that I awoke, I was being carried up a
walk to a rather large, white house with brown trim.
On their side of the walk, bright flowers nodded. A
green lawn stretched from one fence to the other. It
looked like a delightful place to play. I blinked at the

bright sunlight. It was the boy who was carrying me
again.

"Put him down on the grass and I'll get some milk,"
the girl told him.

He put me down and lay down beside me. I tugged
at his shirt sleeve the way that I always tugged at Bruno
II or Treena's ear or tail. The boy giggled and playfully pushed me around with his hand. I growled, a
pretend growl, and wrestled his fingers. He laughed
again and I went for his brown head of hair. I managed
to get a mouthful and tugged — bracing myself to pull.
He put his arms up to protect himself from my make-
believe fury and shrieked with laughter.

His sister returned with the milk and I realized, as I
pushed my nose into the dish, just how thirsty I was.
I drank all of it and stood there with my bulging sides
heaving.

"I don't think that we should play with him when
he's so full," said the girl.

"Let's fix his bed. Maybe he wants to sleep for awhile."

I tried to dance around them to start a game going
again but I was just too full. My tummy felt that it would
pull me to the ground each time that I made a jump.
Though my legs said "up" my stomach said "down"
and finally I decided to obey it and fell right where I
was, my head on my paws. The boy laughed and picked
me up carefully.

"Ate too much, did you? Next time we won't give
you so much all at once."

They fixed an old coat in a big cardboard box and
placed me on it. It felt so good just to crawl off and
close my eyes; still I missed the feel of warm, soft fur.
I had always slept with my head on either Mama or one
of my sisters or brothers. I whimpered once or twice
and then I fell asleep.

When I finally awakened the family was just finishing
dinner. My "training" stood me in good stead and I
whined to leave my box. The mother spoke.

"Mark, I think that you should put the puppy outside for awhile."

He carried me out and placed me on the grass.

"Away you go."

I scampered off. It was awhile before he came for me again. When he did come, the girl came with him. They sat together stroking me and discussing their new pup.

"What shall we call it?"

"Maybe Dusty."

"Naw."

"Lady?"

"I think it's a boy."

"Sandy then? That's his color."

I made a quick grab for shoe laces and bounced back on all fours, then I braced myself, and growling and gurgling, I began to wrestle the enemy strings. Mark laughed.

"I know, Tracy. Let's call him Spunky."

I wasn't even surprised. Of course I was Spunky. That had been my name from birth. I wondered why it had taken them so long to figure it out. I was glad that they finally discovered it.

I left the shoe laces and attacked Mark's pant leg. He took a few steps, dragging me along behind him, then stopped and scooped me up.

"Let's teach him tricks," shouted the girl. "I'll get a ball."

She ran to the house and returned with a small red and blue ball. They sat on the ground a few feet apart and rolled the ball back and forth. It looked like fun. I made a dash for the ball but only managed to knock it away. Back and forth went the ball, and back and forth I went too. The children laughed at my clumsy efforts, and then to my great surprise I managed to sink my teeth into the softness of the ball and it stopped rolling. I picked it up from the ground and made a dash for the flower bed. The children ran after me, laughing and shouting. I waited for them to get near to me and then whirled and dodged away, carrying the ball with me. Round and round we went, until we were all exhausted. I finally flopped down on my tummy and let the girl take the ball from my mouth.

"You're 'spose to bring it back," she chided.

They began to roll the ball again. I couldn't resist. As tired as I was, I just had to be a part of the game. I dashed after the ball. I caught it sooner this time, and when I did, I headed at once for the shrubbery.

"Spunky, come back."

They caught me again and took the ball from my mouth.

Over and over we played the game. It began to dawn on me that after I caught the ball, they wanted it back so that they could roll it for me again. It seemed a rather silly, backward way of doing things. The next time that I caught it, instead of running away, I took the ball straight to Mark.

"He did it. He did it," they both shouted. "He brought back the ball."

If I had known how excited they would get over a little thing like a returned ball, I would have brought it back to them much sooner.

We went on with our game. It was getting cooler now for the sun had swung low in the sky. The lady called.

"Mark and Tracy. It's already past your bedtime. Enough play for tonight. Hurry now."

"Aw Mom."

"We're playing."

"You can play tomorrow. Come now."

Tracy picked me up and we all started for the door.

"We'd better feed him again before we put him to bed."

They fed me, then carried me along as they washed themselves and brushed their teeth. They changed into their pajamas and Tracy scolded Mark for leaving his clothes scattered all over the floor. It reminded me of

Treena's bossiness. A wave of loneliness washed over me. Mark picked up his scattered clothes, wadded them in an unattractive ball and placed them on a chair, then he carried me to my bed with Tracy following.

"While I fix his bed, you put him out once more," Tracy said.

Mark did.

When I came back in, Tracy had my bed all prepared. They put me in it and expected me to snuggle right down and go to sleep. I should have too, after all of the exhausting play, but already I felt that the box was going to be very lonely. I whimpered.

"Now Spunky. It's time to go to sleep."

Tracy reached a hand in and patted me. "Lie down now." But I didn't lie down. I stood on my hind legs with my front paws against the side of the box and pleaded with my eyes and voice for them to please take me with them, whimpering and crying as I tried to scratch my way up and out.

"Aw, you poor puppy," said Mark. "You're lonesome aren't you? It's alright. We'll be right here. It's okay. Go to sleep now."

He put me back on the old coat in the box and pushed me down, stroking me so that I would stay there. I settled in, liking the feeling of the soft hand on my fur. As soon as the petting stopped, I popped up. The children were quietly tip-toeing from the kitchen. I leaped at the side of the box and started to cry again. Back they came.

We repeated this a few times and finally the father came in.

"I thought that your mother said 'bed time.'"

"But he's lonesome."

"He cries when we go."

The father bent over my box. I looked at him with soft pleading in my eyes, not sure how he would respond. He reached out and caressed my silky sides. I licked his hand and shivered my tail to a wiggle.

"Sure he's lonesome. He'll be lonesome for a few nights, but then he'll be okay. He's just got to learn."

He hesitated a moment and then said, "Just wait here a minute."

He was soon back carrying a funny object with him.

"What are you gonna do with that?" asked Mark.

"Put it in his box."

"A dog needs an alarm clock?" asked Tracy, incredulously.

"Not to wake up by — to sleep with," answered the father. "Notice the tick-tick sound. He misses being with his mother. The clock's ticking will remind him of her heartbeat and he'll feel more at home."

He knelt down and arranged the clock under my old coat and then snuggled me down with my head near it and stroked my side with a long gentle finger.

"Off you two go now."

"I sure hope it works."

"So do I."

The two children left and the father stayed a few more minutes, rubbing my side. I sighed contentedly, listening to the soft tick, tick under my head. It was comforting to have the steady beat there but I still missed the warmth of my mother. I even missed the wiggling and the snapping of my brothers and sisters, but oh, I was so tired. I finally let my eyelids close and I guess I fell asleep.

Chapter 7

Alone

When I awoke the house was quiet and only the light from an outside street lamp lighted the kitchen. I pushed around in my box in search of my mother and then realized, with a start, that I was all alone. It came back to me then, and I remembered where I was. Ignoring the soft tick of the clock I bounded up and began to cry and to scratch at the side of my box. The lady soon came. She lifted me gently, talking to me; then she carried me to the door and set me down on the back step.

"You hurry now," she said.

I hurried.

When we got back in the house she put me back in my box. I didn't want to stay alone and began to cry. Her hand went to my head.

"It's okay now. You have to go back to sleep. Lie down now. Come on."

I let her push me down on my bed but when she walked away I was still whimpering.

I slept fitfully for the rest of the night. When I lay awake, the loneliness settled in all around me like a heavy, suffocating blanket. I wanted my Mama with all of my being. I wished that they had brought her too. I liked this new family and would have been happy with them if only I had my mother. Even Treena or Bruno II would have been a great comfort. I thought of Little Majesty and Minx and wondered if they were in some box somewhere all alone, and crying for the rest of the family too.

I would sleep for a short while and then awaken again, to lie shivering and whimpering. I wanted to go home.

The sun was just showering brand new rays of light into the kitchen when Mark appeared. He picked me up from my box. Never had I been so happy to see a human. My whole body quivered and I kissed his cheek, his hair, his nose, his ear, over and over again. He giggled.

He put me outside for awhile, then took me to his room with him. We settled down in his big bed. I snuggled up close against his pajamaed chest. I could hear the soft tick-tick of his heart and feel the warmth coming from his body. I curled up close and made up for some of the sleep that I had missed during the night.

Chapter 8

Happening

July 6 — My new family is okay. I still miss Mama and
Bruno II and Treena. I miss Little Majesty and Minx
too, but I like Mr. and Mrs. Dobson and I love Tracy
and Mark. There are two others who live here too. They
are to come home from camp in a few days.

July 8 — I'm getting really good at chasing a ball
now — and catching it. I get loved everytime when I
bring it back. Today Mark and I played with a stick.
I think that he wants me to chase it too. It doesn't roll.
Sometimes when I pick it up, one end drags on the
ground. I don't know why Mark plays with it when we
could use a ball, but if he likes it then I guess I can put
up with it if it will amuse him.

I still miss Mama.

July 10 — I have a nice big yard to play in but Mrs.
Dobson is sure fussy about her flowerbeds. She shoos
me out everytime I go in them. They are so much fun
to hide and to wrestle around in. I do wish that she
wouldn't get so upset about them.

I sleep a little better.

July 25 — Two more family members came home today, an older boy named Grant — he's twelve, and a girl Sandra, aged nine. They approved of me.

With four people to hold me, I hardly got to try out my legs. I was glad for a chance to run and explore on my own while they were having their dinner.

July 29 — I heard Mr. Dobson warning all of the children to be sure to keep the gates closed tightly. I wonder if I were to leave the yard if I'd be able on my own to find Mama. I think maybe I could. It makes me feel all excited just to think about it. There was no chance to try today. They closed the gate carefully each time that they came or went.

Aug. 20 — The kids were all talking about "school" today. I don't know what school is but they all sounded excited so I guess it must be something fun. They talked of "getting ready for it" and "having their supplies for it," and about "going to it." I sure hope that they will take me too.

Chapter 9

The Stolen Ball

Aug. 21 — Yesterday Mark took me for a run down the alley and into the playground. It was lots of fun. There were other kids there too and they all wanted to hold me. I wanted to run.

Some boys were playing with a great big, brown ball. I tried to catch it but I couldn't even get my mouth on it. They just laughed at me.

Some smaller kids were playing in a big box with dirt in it.

They were building roads and pushing small cars and trucks back and forth. One boy had a truck that could carry loads of dirt. He'd fill it up and then push it over to the side of the box by the swing, and dump all of the dirt out into a big pile. I started to dig in the dirt but I guess it was right in the middle of one of their roads 'cause they started to yell at me. Mark called, "C'mon Spunky — out of the sandbox," so I went with him to the slide.

He held me on his lap and we went down again and again. Mark seemed to really like the slide and I guess he thought that I did too, but I wasn't sure. It was so high up in the air and the fast whoosh made my tummy feel funny. I was glad when Mark went to play on the swing and I could explore on my own.

I couldn't believe my good luck. I found a ball. It was all blue and was a little bigger than our ball at home but I was able to get it in my mouth. I could hardly wait to show Mark. He was so fond of rolling a ball that I was sure he would really be excited about it.

I picked up the ball and pranced across the cool, green grass, looking for Mark. He was playing some kind of a wrestling game with another boy and I had to drop the ball and pull on his pant leg to get his attention. He finally noticed me and stopped rolling on the ground. He sat up and brushed the grass from his T-shirt. I chose that moment to pick up the ball and proudly present it to him, but he didn't sound pleased when he spoke.

"Where'd you get that, Spunky?"

I wagged my tail and dropped the ball in his lap, in a hurry for him to start our game. He jumped up.

"Where'd you find it, Spunky? That's not your ball. Don't you know that it's wrong to take something that isn't yours?"

I must have looked as perplexed as I felt, for he reached down and put a hand on my head. Even though his hand felt gentle, his voice did not change.

"It's not your ball, Spunky. You took someone else's ball. That's stealing, Spunky — to take something that isn't yours. It's wrong to steal, Spunky. Someone else will be looking for his ball and he'll feel sad when he can't find it. I wish that I knew where you got it so that I could take it back. You must never, never do that again Spunky, do you hear?"

I heard. I hadn't meant to do wrong. I was sorry that I had taken someone else's ball which would make him feel sad. I was sorry that I had done something that made Mark feel angry. I lowered my head and whined.

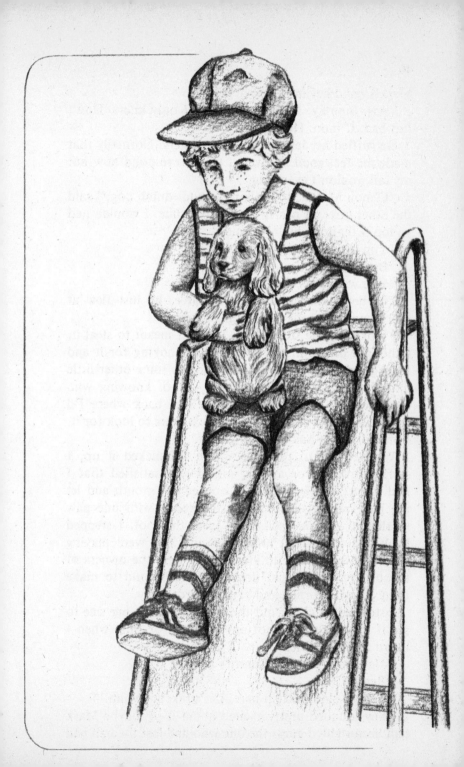

Mark's hand began to stroke me.

"Aw, Spunky. It's done now. If I only knew. Don't feel bad. C'mon. Here boy."

He ruffled my left ear with his fingers. Normally that made me feel good all over. I tried to respond now but my tail wouldn't even wag.

"C'mon Mark. Stop talkin' to your dumb dog," said the other boy. "I nearly got ya that time. I woulda had ya too if that dog hadn't come."

"You would not," stated Mark.

"Bet I woulda."

"You wanna try again?"

The boy didn't even wait to agree, he just flew at Mark and they went to wrestling again.

I looked at the stolen ball. I hadn't meant to steal it. I thought of the kids who would be looking for it and feeling sad. Maybe it even belonged to some other little dog. I couldn't find the owners — not knowing who they were — but I could put the ball back where I'd found it. Maybe they would go back there to look for it. I picked up the ball and started off.

When I got to the area where I'd picked it up, I sniffed around for awhile until I was satisfied that I had found the right place. I opened my mouth and let the ball fall on the ground, stopping it with one paw so that it wouldn't roll away from the spot. I stepped back and looked all around. Some kids were playing not far away. I had no idea if they were the owners of the ball or not. I had done all that I could to make things right. I turned and began to trot away.

I stopped to check out the grass around a big tree to see if it had the scent of any squirrels or cats, when I heard a happy shriek.

"Hey look — here's Kenny's ball."

"Really?"

"Yeah — look. Right here. Let's take it to him."

They sounded pretty excited about it so maybe Mark had been right. I guess the one who had lost the ball had felt sad and would now be happy when the ball was returned. I was glad that I had taken the trouble to put the ball back. I wished that there were some way that I could tell Mark. No matter how hard I tried, I couldn't get him to understand my language. Oh, he understood some things, like when I wanted a drink or my food or to go outside or to play, but often what I really wanted to share with him, just didn't get through. I suppose that humans can't help it if they don't have the intelligence that dogs have. I understand Mark perfectly.

Well even though I wouldn't be able to tell Mark all about it, I felt so much better about having taken the ball back to where it belonged. I determined that I'd never take something that wasn't mine again.

I picked up my ears and frisked my tail as I went looking for Mark. My stomach was telling me that it was getting near dinner time. I hoped that Mark was finished wrestling and was ready to go home.

Chapter 10

Lessons

Aug. 22 — Mrs. Dobson does not like me on the living room carpet. She is repeatedly telling the kids to keep me out of the room. I try to stay out but it is so easy to forget when they all are in there. Tonight Sandra was practicing piano and Tracy and Mark were stretched out on the floor playing a game. I just wanted to watch them for awhile so I sneaked in bit by bit.

I was sure that I hadn't been noticed, when — smack. The noise was enough to deafen one and I felt a whack on my behind. It didn't hurt really, but it frightened me half to death. With one wild yelp, I headed for the kitchen and my box. Normally I was unable to get either in or out of my box on my own, but I guess my fright carried me up and over the top, for before I realized what had happened, I was burrowing into my old coat, trying to hide and find comfort at the same time.

I later discovered that the "weapon" used to discipline me was a rolled up newspaper. It really worked — if scaring one nearly out of his wits was the purpose. I have no desire to experience that again. Mrs. Dobson

can have her carpet all to herself.

Aug. 25 — A lot of things were happening yesterday. Mark and Grant got up early and left on a fishing trip with their dad. I wanted to go too but they decided against it.

Tracy had a friend in to spend the day with her; Sandra had a piano lesson and then went off to the swimming pool.

It wasn't the *normal* Saturday and somehow the daily routine got all mixed up.

Mark and Grant were too excited to think of anything but their fishing, so when I got up and went to my dish for my breakfast it was empty.

I distinctly heard Mrs. Dobson tell the girls to be sure that they fed me before they ran off, but I guess they forgot. I checked my dish once or twice during the morning but it was still empty. I decided that I'd just have to tough it out until lunch time; then they would surely remember, but somehow I was missed again.

My stomach was empty and hurting as I lay out in the backyard that afternoon. I chewed on my chewing-bones but there wasn't any relief there. I finished the small amount of water in my water dish but that really didn't take the gnawing feeling away. It seemed a long time until the family gathered for the evening meal. The menfolk still weren't home from their fishing so the ladies ate alone. I waited by my dish hoping that some-one would notice me, but they hurried through their dinner; then Mrs. Dobson busied herself with the dishes and the girls ran off.

I stood by my dish and whined but no one even noticed. I finally crawled into a corner and tried to sleep. It didn't work. My stomach was too empty. Mrs. Dobson didn't understand why I whined and first she thought that I wanted out — then back in again. She didn't realize that my problem was hunger.

The girls were called from their play and sent to bed and Mrs. Dobson started to watch the clock. She was anxious for the boys and Mr. Dobson to return from fishing.

We finally heard the car drive in and the boys ran in excitedly. They were full of the news of the fishing trip — about the ones that they caught and the ones that got away. They were soon shooed off to the bathroom to prepare for bed. I tried to tell Mark that I hadn't been fed all day but he thought that I was trying to tell him that I had missed him — which I had, but, oh, how my poor stomach growled and groaned.

The boys went to bed and I was told to go to bed too. I tried. Really I tried. I lay down on my bed and shut my eyes, but my empty tummy ached to be fed. I whined and was put out. I cried and was brought back in. I cried some more and was scolded and put in my box.

I curled up and tried to settle down but my stomach hurt too much. I felt sure that I would die of hunger long before the sun came up again. I shifted my position, this way, that way, but it didn't help. I whined and cried. Mr. Dobson came.

"Now Spunky," he said crossly, "that's enough. What's the matter with you anyway? Now you settle down and go to sleep — do you hear? I don't want to hear any more fussing."

He gave me a cuff on my rear and I knew that I had to be quiet. It didn't hurt really, but it did let me know that Mr. Dobson meant business.

I crawled over into the far corner of my box and was quiet. Oh, how my stomach hurt. It rolled and pinched and picked at me. Finally I was able to doze off, only to waken again with more hunger pains. I thought that morning would never come but it eventually did, and with it came Tracy.

"Hi Spunky," she called and lifted me from my box. I ran immediately to my dish.

"Are you hungry?"

She opened a tin of food and put some in my dish

and I dug in, fairly falling into the food in my eagerness.

"Oh Spunky," she laughed, "Are you *that* hungry?"

I didn't stop to tell her that I certainly was.

Sandra came in.

"Look how hungry Spunky is." Tracy pointed a finger at me as I wolfed down my food. Sandra stood with a frown on her face.

"Did you feed him yesterday?" she finally asked.

"Didn't you?"

"I forgot."

"So did I," said Tracy slowly.

They exchanged looks.

"That's why he was crying." Sandra spoke slowly and thoughtfully.

"Oh Spunky." Tracy sounded about to cry. "I'm so sorry. I'll never forget you again. Never."

She stroked me as I ate.

"Now don't eat too fast or you'll get a tummy ache."

I didn't see how my stomach could possibly hurt more than it already had.

"That's enough for now," said Sandra, lifting me up. "You go outside for awhile and a little later you can have some more."

She put me out and I flopped down on the grass and licked the last bits of food off my chops. In a few minutes my stomach began to feel comfortable again. I was glad that I had been stopped from eating any more for the present. I even forgave the girls for not feeding me, even if I had suffered horribly and had feared that I wouldn't last the night. I forgave — but I hoped with all of my heart that it would never happen again.

I guess a dog needs to have a lot of faith in his humans.

Chapter 11

Church

Aug. 25 — Every Sunday the family goes off to Church and I have to remain at home all alone. They seem to enjoy Church and are always excited about going and happy when they return. It didn't really seem fair to me. I like fun things too.

On Sundays when the weather was bad my box was moved into the back entry and placed on its side so that I could come and go as I pleased. My water dish was placed there for me and also whatever was left over from my breakfast. I even had my store-bought chewing toys so I didn't suffer any.

On nice days I was allowed to stay out of doors. Again my water dish was filled for me and my toys were laid out. Still, I felt cheated. What I wanted was to be able to go to Church too.

The Church is nearby. I knew that, for often on the nice sunny days the family chooses to walk to Church rather than to take the car.

It seemed that I had waited at home all alone for many, many Sundays feeling bored and pouty. I knew within myself that at the first opportunity, I was going to Church too.

Today was a warm, summer day with an ever-so-slight breeze blowing. The summer flowers were at the height of their blooming and a few butterflies floated aimlessly back and forth from flowerbed to flowerbed.

The family left for Church a bit early so that they could enjoy the walk, and I was placed in the backyard with only my water dish and chewing bone for company. My ball was lying there but it was no fun without someone to throw it for me. I didn't feel like chewing. I sulked for awhile, then finally gave that up and went to wrestle the flowers in Mrs. Dobson's flowerbeds and send a few butterflies scurrying away. Time passed slowly. I tired of the game and rested on the cool grass. I was aroused by the sound of children on the sidewalk and thought that maybe my family was coming home, but when I peeked out of the wire fence I discovered that it was some kids that I didn't know. It was company anyway, and the sight of them filled me with excitement and I bounced and barked and wagged my tail and coaxed them to come and play with me. They came — through the gate, into the backyard — exclaiming over and over about the cute puppy.

We rolled and played on the grass for quite awhile. I showed them how to roll and catch a ball and I thought that they would never tire of the game.

All too soon though, they decided that they should go, so the game stopped. I went over for a much needed drink and they disappeared down the sidewalk, calling goodby as they went.

It wasn't until after they were gone that I noticed the gate. It was open just a crack. I could hardly believe my good luck and before there was any chance of something happening to close it, I dashed through and out to the sidewalk. Now I could go to Church.

I knew the direction that the Dobsons went and that was enough. With my nose to the ground I passed back and forth across the sidewalk sniffing for signs to guide me. Now and then I caught a whiff of the smell of one of the Dobsons and that led me on.

I soon came to a large building with many cars parked around it. This must be Church I reasoned, and, sure enough, when I reached the steps I caught a distinct whiff of Mark at the railing.

I went on up the steps but the door was closed. I rattled at it and soon it was opened, rather cautiously and curiously, I thought, and a tall man dressed in a dark blue suit looked out.

As soon as he spotted me he started to close the door again but I managed to slip through just in time. I had to quickly tuck in my tail so that the fast-closing door didn't catch it.

The man spoke quickly to another man standing by an inner door and that man turned to face me, bending over to pick me up.

"Here doggie — nice doggie." He spoke in a whisper.

I wasn't to be fooled. If this man had his way I would probably be stuck there playing with him for hours. As nice as he seemed, I didn't want to play just then. I wanted to find Mark. I hated to disappoint him completely though, so I pranced toward him, dodged back, and pranced toward him again. When he reached out for me I gave a sharp bark and jumped aside, happy to take the time to play a little before going to find Mark. The man made a grab for me but missed. I ran between his legs and through the next doors. I heard the man scrambling behind me but I had already spent enough time playing so I headed under the many seats that stretched out before me.

All I could see were legs and shoes — lots and lots of them — but none of them looked like they belonged to members of my family. I finally saw one pair of shoes that looked like a pair that Mrs. Dobson wore, but when I sniffed at it to see if it were she, a lady screamed —a tight, controlled little scream — and jumped like I had bitten her. I could feel a general stir throughout all of the legs. Some were lifted right off the floor and out of sight. I withdrew to where I considered myself safe and waited for the legs to start coming back down to their rightful positions.

After a few moments I sneaked a peak out from under the bench. There was a wide aisle with seats filled with people on either side. Down at the end of the aisle on a raised platform, stood a man talking to the people.

I was just wondering if I should go down and speak to him when I saw the door-man and the play-man coming slowly down the aisle, peering first to the right, then to the left. At the same time I noticed someone in the seats opposite me who looked like Mark. I decided to make a dash for him.

As soon as my nose showed, the play-man rushed forward and reached for me. The door-man spotted me too and now he also wanted to play. I hated to disappoint them when they were both so nice. If I'd had time I would have played with them, but first I wanted to let Mark know that I had joined him at Church.

I dodged around the play-man and into the aisle. The men both lunged for me at the same time but instead of getting me, they got all tangled up with one another. The play-man landed right on his tummy in the middle of the aisle, a funny grunt coming from him as he hit the carpet. I heard a child shriek, "Doggie," in a happy voice but I didn't even stop to say hello.

I found Mark. "Spunky," he whispered and put a hand down to clutch my collar and hopefully silence my excitement.

The man at the front had stopped speaking. He was looking at the two men still in the aisle with a confused look on his face. The man with the glasses had managed to find them and was struggling up from his knees. The other man was also getting up, carefully smoothing out his suit. Both men had very red faces. Six faces looked down at me and they too were turning red.

The man at the front spoke again and there was a smile in his voice.

"It seems that we have a 'visitor' with us this morning. I'm sorry gentlemen about your little accident. If someone is able to successfully catch our little 'guest,' he has my permission to remove him quietly."

I wiggled against Mark. Mr. Dobson whispered huskily, "Mark, pick him up and take him home."

Mark held me firmly and took me from the Church.

I was disappointed. I had found Mark — for that I was thankful — but I had so much wanted to spend more time at Church. It was a fun place all right — all of those people playing games, and that man at the front with the laughter in his voice. No wonder my family enjoyed Church so.

I hope that I will be able to go again, but I suppose that the gate will be doubly secured from now on.

Chapter 12

Nero

Aug. 28 — I was in my backyard today when I noticed a stirring in the garden next door. I stood watching carefully. Sneaking along among the carrot tops was a sleek black something. It seemed to be making its way toward a robin who was quite oblivious to it all as she pecked and tugged at an earthworm in the potato patch.

It finally dawned on me that the "something" was a cat, and that he was intent on catching that robin. A pair of robins had decided to build a nest in our spruce tree earlier in the year. Their young were on their own now, but they still hung around our yard a lot. These robins belonged to *my* family and that big black cat had no business at all creeping up on me.

Just as the cat was ready to spring I ran at the fence barking and jumping. It had the desired effect. The startled bird flew away. It must have wondered why I suddenly turned enemy after being its friend — unless of course it had spotted the black cat and realized what had nearly happened.

The robin flew to a nearby tree and sat scolding

crossly, probably thinking of the fat earthworm that got away. The cat stretched itself up to its full height and gave me a withering look. I had interferred with his hunting and it was plain that he was not at all pleased about it. I didn't back down but accused him crossly, "That's our robin — you leave it alone."

He seemed to grow even bigger — perhaps because his hair was standing on end.

"No robin," he spat out, "is *your* robin. You don't even eat robins, so how can you call it yours?"

"It's my family's," I continued, "and robins are *not* to eat."

"Oh yeah," said the cat savagely, "and what *are* they for?"

"To watch."

"To watch. That's the craziest thing I've ever heard. Who ever filled their stomach by watching?"

"You don't need that robin to fill your stomach. You have a family. They feed you."

"They want me to earn my keep. I'm supposed to hunt."

"Not robins."

"And why not robins?" He was still angry with me.

"Robins don't hurt anything. My people like them."

"And your people do not have a strawberry patch."

I could sense that we were getting nowhere. The cat was still spitting mad and I was upset too.

"Your family keeps the strawberries covered when there are berries there," I countered.

He gave me a dirty look.

"They wouldn't have to go to all of that work if it weren't for the robins," he said.

I was tired of the argument. He was still bristling anyway. I decided to try for peace.

"If you're really hungry," I said, "there's food in my dish. You can have it if you like."

He looked at me disdainfully.

"I'm not *that* hungry," he said and turned his back

on me and began licking his paw and washing his face. I lowered myself to the cool grass and lay watching him.

He seemed to get over his anger after awhile but he still ignored me. I finally found the courage to approach him again.

"What's your name?"

He hesitated and I thought that maybe he wouldn't answer me at all, but at length he straightened up and stared directly at me and pride puffed him up as he spoke the one word "Nero."

"Nero," I echoed. I guessed that it must be a pretty special name the way that he acted about it; still, I had never heard of anyone named that before.

"And don't forget it," he said arrogantly. He stood up. "And remember this too, Pup — we are stuck here as neighbors. I guess that there's not much that we can do about that, but if there's not to be trouble then it's best that we stay out of one another's hair — understand? You leave me alone — I leave you alone — see?"

I think I understood quite clearly what he was trying to say but I pretended to be dumb.

"Meaning?"

"Meaning," said the black Nero, "that if you stick your nose in my business, you get it scratched."

He fairly hissed out the last word and giving me one last, hateful look, he stretched to his full height and started for his back porch.

"And you leave our robins alone too," I called after him.

He turned to glare at me and then he sprang lightly to the porch rail and dropped down on the other side. So much for neighborliness, I thought.

He hadn't been gone long when my thoughts began to untangle from my angry feelings. If I were a cat, and a pup chased away my dinner, I guessed I'd be a little angry too. I lay down again and chewed on my chew-stick while I thought it all out. Maybe Nero had a right to be mad — and we were neighbors. I decided that I'd apologize the next time that I saw him — maybe — just a little bit. At least I'd try to be a bit more agreeable.

I pushed away my chew-stick and headed for my back door. I decided that I'd forgive Nero and forget the whole thing. I'm sure that it is much more agreeable if one gets on well with his neighbors.

Chapter 13

School

Sept. 1 — School. I've heard that word so often in the last few days. The kids are all so excited about it that I can hardly wait to go. They have books and pencils and crayons all laid out ready to take with them. They have shiny new lunch boxes with their names on them too. Tracy even has her new shirt and jeans all laid out on her bed, and Mark has new joggers all ready to step into. Guess I'll just have to go as I am.

Sept. 2 — Today has seemed a hundred years long and I am so exhausted that I can hardly hold up my head. Never again do I want to repeat the experiences that were mine today — but I should start from the beginning.

As soon as the children were up — and that was much earlier than usual — the house just buzzed with activity and excitement. I could hardly contain myself and rushed back and forth from room to room, jumping, and barking short excited barks as I watched everyone getting ready for school. I could hardly wait to get started. Do you know what they did with the shiny lunch boxes? They packed them with sandwiches and fruit and chocolate chip cookies and milk. I didn't see them put in the dog food, but I didn't mind sharing chocolate chip cookies and milk.

They had breakfast and everyone was so excited that they could hardly eat. I gulped my food quickly and then waited by the door.

Finally everyone seemed ready to go. They stood in their new clothes, holding their new lunch boxes and their bags of school supplies, watching the clock and the street in front of their house by turn. Mrs. Dobson laughed.

"You're ready way too early," she said. "Now you'll have to stand and wait."

They laughed too, but they got really fidgety just standing there. I couldn't understand why we didn't just go.

Finally after what seemed an awfully long time Mark cried, "There it comes." A yellow bus came down the street.

They all shouted goodby to their mother and hurried to the door. For a moment I wondered why they didn't feel sad, as I had, about leaving their mother. They all loved her, I knew, and yet they seemed to feel only excitement about going off to School and leaving her behind. I couldn't understand why she didn't come too. I knew that I would miss her. I stopped just long enough to look at her and whimper. That was my mistake. The children hurried through the door and as I went to scurry after them, Grant stopped me.

"Spunky, you can't go," he said.

He picked me up and handed me to Mrs. Dobson. "You'd better hold him until we're gone."

She took me and closed the door firmly behind the disappearing children with a last call of goodby. I couldn't believe it. Surely they had planned to take me along. There must be some mistake, I thought. I had been excited too. I had hurried through breakfast to be ready. I had washed myself as carefully as I could — and who was going to drink all of that milk?

I squirmed, trying to get out of Mrs. Dobson's arms, barking and wiggling in my agitation. She just held me closer and crossed to a window, carrying me directly over that forbidden carpet with no thought at all.

There were all four children waiting on the sidewalk for the yellow bus to draw up beside them. It did, and the driver opened the funny, folding door. They scampered up the steps, too excited to even turn and look back at the house. From where we stood I could hear glad cries as they called to friends.

I lurched in Mrs. Dobson's arms. I had to hurry or it would be too late for them to realize their mistake — they had forgotten me.

Mrs. Dobson's hands held me firmly. "Now Spunky," she said. "You are going to have to get used to it. They must go to school now. Summer playtime is over. You'll miss them I know. I'll miss them too."

She put me down and I ran to the door and whined. When she paid no attention to the whining I began to scratch.

"Now Spunky," she scolded. "None of that. I don't want the door all scratched up. Come on, be a good dog. You can't go with them."

She scooped me up and scratched my ear to distract me; then she deposited me in my box.

"Now lay down for awhile and take a nap. The day will go faster that way. Be a good dog now. They'll be home before you know it."

It hit me then. I really wasn't going to be allowed to go to school. Humans thought that School was for children, not dogs — like Church. But how did Mrs. Dobson know that I wouldn't like it. I had liked Church, not that it had changed anything; I still wasn't allowed to return. Maybe I'd like School too if I were just given a chance.

I was glad to hear that the children weren't going to

stay at school, that they'd come home again. I guessed that that was the reason why they hadn't minded leaving their mother and me, but I still felt lonesome. The house was so quiet and Mrs. Dobson didn't play much.

She busied herself with the noisy vacuum cleaner and I crawled into the farthest corner of my box and tried to sleep. There was no use whining — the vacuum cleaner was so loud that she wouldn't hear me anyway, but I couldn't sleep either — not with all of that racket. I finally gave up on both and just lay there feeling sorry for myself.

Mrs. Dobson turned off the noisy machine after what seemed like an awfully long time. I wondered if it were time for the children to come home from School yet. I stood up on my hind legs, scratched at my box, and whined.

"Would you like out for awhile?" Mrs. Dobson asked, as she lifted me gently out of the box and carried me to the door.

"There you go. Go and play for awhile."

I waited for the door to close and then ran straight for the gate. Perhaps Mark had left it open for me so that I could follow him to School. But no. It was closed tightly and the latch held firm when I jumped against it and pushed with all of my might.

In a frenzy I ran round and round the yard, looking for some way out. If only I could get away I was sure that I could find the big yellow bus that was taking the children to School.

Just as I was about to give up I remembered the flowerbeds. The dirt was soft there. I had often dug just for fun, but if I could dig a hole under the fence I might be able to squeeze myself through it. I went right to work and sure enough, in next to no time, I was able to wiggle and squirm my way under the fence.

I raced to the sidewalk. The yellow bus was nowhere in sight. I stood for a moment to get my bearings and then began to run in the direction that I had seen it go.

I put my nose to the ground hoping for some scent to guide me but there was just a confusing mixture of tire, exhaust, and concrete smells. I would have to go by instinct alone.

I ran for a long way, until my sides were heaving and my tongue lolling out, but still the yellow bus evaded me. I was forced to slow my pace. My heart was pounding in my chest as though it would hammer its way right through my skin. I wondered if I should turn around and go home and just wait out the long day until the children returned, but the thought was not a welcome one. I wanted so much to find them, to go to School, to share in their excitement — so I just kept slowly plodding along.

Chapter 14

Lost

Sept. 2, con't. — I decided to try a side street. Maybe the big yellow bus had turned. I turned to my right at the next corner and travelled rather slowly down a street lined with houses.

As I passed one of them I heard a stir and looked up to see a huge dog make a lunge for me. My heart stopped short and I fairly fell in my tracks feeling that surely this was the end of me. He was so big and looked so angry and the growl that came from his throat sounded so vicious.

I shut my eyes to block out the whole scene. I didn't want to see myself picked up, shaken like a rag, and then thrown down again on the sidewalk.

There was a heavy, crashing sound and I opened my eyes just a fraction. The big dog had smacked up against a tall, wire fence, and wonder of wonders, it was holding him. He threw himself at it again and again and still it held.

I struggled to my shaky feet and started off down the sidewalk gathering momentum as I ran. I glanced over

my shoulder occasionally to see if that fence were still doing its job. It was. I was safe. I decided right then and there to get out of that area as quickly as I could, and I ran, almost blindly, crossing the wide street as though that big dog were right at my heels. Horns honked, tires screeched and men yelled at me from fast moving cars. I barely escaped one set of wheels and my hair stood on end with the horror of it all. It was almost more than I could take, and as soon as I reached the safety of the green grass beyond the sidewalk, I crawled beneath a low growing shrub and flopped down on the ground, panting and heaving and shaking with fright. My sides ached, my feet hurt, and I was scared and thirsty. I lay as quietly as I could, wondering what to do next. The blood pounded in my brain so that I could hardly think. I decided that for now my only recourse was to rest until I could think straight again. Later I would figure out what I should do. How I longed for a cool drink. My tongue seemed much too big for my mouth. I felt like it would never feel cool again. I closed my eyes and lay still for a long time.

Gradually my sides stopped heaving and my body cooled down. I was still thirsty. I needed a drink badly but I wasn't sure where to find one. I just couldn't stay where I was. I had to find either the yellow bus or School — or else return home.

I crawled out from under the cool shrub and began a slow trot down the sidewalk. The sun was high in the sky now and my tummy was telling me that it was past lunch time. There didn't seem to be anything around to eat though, not even a drink.

I found a place where the smell of good food hung heavily in the air. A few people were sitting outside at tables, eating. Mama had taught all of us not to beg at the table, so I hung back until the people were finished and then hurried forward. I nosed around under the table but all that I found was one stepped upon french fry. There was no water.

More people came. I waited for them to finish eating. Again they left nothing much behind. Other people came and went. Still no food was put out for me. I decided that if I were to be fed, I must make them aware that I was there — and hungry, so I went up to a table where two men sat. I didn't beg really, I just pushed against one of the men's legs so that he would notice me. He did — but he didn't share his lunch. Instead he chased me away and when I was reluctant to go he threw small, gravelly stones at me. I left then, knowing that I wouldn't find food there.

The long day dragged on. I was forced to give up on finding the yellow bus or School and decided to go home. I hated to admit defeat but I was so thirsty and so tired that home sounded awfully good — so I set out.

I hadn't gone far when I realized that I wasn't going home at all. I was helplessly, hopelessly lost. Now what would I do? A funny knot of fear began to tighten my stomach.

Would I ever find my family again? What would I do for food? Where would I sleep? Near panic took hold of me. I became desperate. I must find them. I must.

All of the long afternoon I searched, up one street, down another, through back alleys and on side streets. Nothing looked familiar. In fact, I became suspicious that my searching was taking me further away, rather than closer to home. Still I would not give up.

I was so thirsty that my thoughts turned momentarily from finding home to finding water. If I were ever to arrive at home I needed water to do so. I trudged on, my eyes and nose searching.

The smell of water drew me to the right and I hurried forward. A lady was watering her front flowers. In thankfulness I made a dash for the spot where the hose was making a small puddle on her front walk. A big orange cat lay stretched out lazily on the porch steps. As I ran toward the water the cat misunderstood my action and jumped to her feet, arching her back and sending forth an exaggerated hiss. I guess the lady thought that I was after her cat too for she turned quickly and pointed the hose directly at me. The cold, hard water splashed full against my face.

"Get out of here. Scram!" she cried and I turned and ran.

I had been so close to a drink and yet had been denied it. I sat down and licked the few remaining drops of wetness from my coat. It helped some but I so much wished that I could stick my nose into a deep dish of cool water or milk and drink and drink.

After I had licked the last of the water from my fur I started on again.

Kids yelled at me, cars honked whenever I crossed the street, dogs barked and growled, cats either turned and ran or else threatened me with outstretched claws. I avoided them all as much as I could and went on looking for my home. I was much more cautious about the traffic now and tried to wait for a lapse of cars before I attempted a crossing. Even so, my heart beat more quickly each time that I saw a curb appearing.

It was getting dark and I ached all over; still I plodded on. I had about given up hope of ever finding my family again and I felt very sad — even sadder, I believe, than when I had left Mama, for now I had no one. Would they miss me? Would Mark feel sorry that he had lost his dog like the boy had felt sad when he lost his ball? I wasn't sure, but somehow I felt that I would be missed.

I was just ready to crawl beneath the shadowy arms of a low shrub on someone's front lawn and cry myself to sleep when I thought that I heard my name. I perked up my ears and listened and I heard it again.

I looked down the street and there came the Dobson's car. Mr. Dobson was driving slowly and Mark and Grant were positioned at open windows, calling at intervals as they came along, "Spunky — here Spunky."

I came alive again and ran toward them barking and wagging my tail. In my excitement I almost forgot to

watch for cars but checked at the last moment and then dashed across the street to the Dobson auto. The car jerked to a stop and Mark jumped out.

He picked me up and held me close — so close that I could hardly wiggle my happiness at seeing him. I was never so glad to see anyone in all of my life. He hugged me and I kissed him, licking his nose, his ear, his cheek —wherever my tongue could get in a lick.

"Oh Spunky, where have you been? We've looked and looked."

I wanted to tell him that I'd looked and looked too but I didn't know how to say it.

"We'd better hurry, Mark," said Mr. Dobson. "Your mother is still waiting our dinner."

We crawled into the car and went home. I was so glad to see my own family, my own house, my own yard, my own bed, but I was so tired that I could hardly stay awake long enough to drink the nice, cool milk and fill my empty tummy. I curled up on the soft old coat in the corner of my box and prepared for sleep.

"I'm afraid that you'll need to get a chain for Spunky and tie him up until he gets used to your going off to school. We don't want this to happen again," said Mr. Dobson.

I wished that I could tell him that he needn't worry, that I would never, never leave home alone again, not even to find the yellow school bus. I much preferred my own home to barking dogs, hissing cats, screeching tires, and cold-water hoses.

I couldn't tell him though, so I just snuggled up contentedly. If they wanted to put me on a chain, that was all right with me.

Chapter 15

The Farm

Sept. 20 — The children have been going to school for some time now. I am always sad to see them go but realize now that they will be home again in a few hours and then they will play with me.

I am getting quite big now, but I still am rather clumsy. Somehow my feet just don't always work the way that I want them to.

Sept. 25 — Mark is really excited. Mr. Dobson announced that on Saturday we will all go to the Farm. All of the children cheered, but Mark seems the happiest of all. His cousins live at the Farm, and he says that he can hardly wait to see them. Mark has promised me that I can go too. I'm glad that it's not like Church or School. I can hardly wait. I've never been to the "Farm" before.

Sept. 27 — Tomorrow is the day that the family goes to the Farm. It must be more like Church than like School because Mr. and Mrs. Dobson are going too. I wonder if we will all go in the big yellow bus. I'm not sure which street the Farm is on.

Sept. 28 — Today I was hauled out of my box before I

even had time to wake up. Mark was so excited about getting to the Farm that he couldn't sleep and so he came for me. He finally raised the rest of the family, and after a hurried breakfast we were ready to go. Mark picked me up and carried me to the car. I was so happy to be able to go with them that I nearly made Mark drop me.

"We're going to the Farm Spunky."

I was rather disappointed not to be able to ride the yellow bus, but I always enjoy a car ride.

The drive was a rather long one but I didn't tire of it. I stood on Mark's lap with my front feet against the window and watched everything that we passed.

We saw a couple of big dogs and I barked at them, feeling quite safe to do so from my position behind glass and in a moving car. It made me feel so good.

We passed right by all of the houses and big buildings of the town and travelled out a busy road with many cars on both sides of us. After awhile there were fewer cars and then we turned and went on a road that didn't have room for other cars to travel on each side of us.

When we arrived at the Farm I was filled with excitement. It was so big and there was so much to see that I could hardly wait to get started. I guess Mark felt that way too, for the car had no sooner stopped than he was out. He was greeted by a boy cousin about his age. After slapping one another on the back a few times, they started off for the barn, talking excitedly as they went. There were other cousins too, and the rest of the Dobson children went off in different directions with them. The older Dobsons were invited in for coffee by the other Dobson grownups.

I stood there watching all of the people disappear and wondering just which way to go first. My nose picked up many new things that I had never smelled before. It twitched in its eagerness to find out just what each new thing was like.

I headed out around the house and nearly ran over a

big brown dog lying in the shade. I stopped short, wondering about the consequence of my actions, but the big dog just gave a careless wag of her tail and went back to sleeping. I felt bolder then and advanced slowly. She was an old dog and not the least inclined to discipline a wayward pup. I tried to encourage her to play when I found that she wasn't cantankerous, but she just ignored me. Friendly though she was, it was plain that she wished to be left alone. Surely I could find something more interesting than visiting with an old dog, even if she were one of my kind, so I left her and went to see what I could find.

I hadn't gone far when I found something with promise. A big multi-colored cat lay stretched out in the sun, quite oblivious to anything around her. Occasionally her tail twitched, or her ear flicked, but, other than that, nothing moved. My encounter with the dog had encouraged me. I advanced toward the cat slowly, silently. My first intention was simply to see if I could make friends with her, but the closer I got the bolder I grew. She lay there so peacefully, so unsuspecting, and suddenly I was overcome with the urge to give her a real start. I wondered if I could pull it off.

Carefully I crept nearer and nearer until I was within striking distance. I could barely contain a gleeful giggle. I waited until I judged that the time was right and then I hurled myself forward, barking with all the force that I could muster. The dead-looking cat sprang to life like a stretched out spring snapped back in coil. She landed on her feet, her back arched, her hair on end, and her green eyes flashing. She didn't even wait to see what I was, or how big a creature I turned out to be. In one giant leap she was off the ground and half-way up a nearby tree.

I was right after her, barking and leaping and feeling proud of myself for having put her to flight. I had never had that kind of an experience with a cat before and found it tremendously exciting.

She wouldn't come back down so that I could chase her again, so after getting bored with waiting and having a throat that ached from barking, I left her and went to see what else I could find.

What I found was a flock of chickens, clucking and pecking their way across the yard. I went racing right into the midst of them, barking wildly. It worked. They fluttered and scattered in every direction, sending feathers and dirt flying as they flew. It was great sport. I chased them around a few more times, enjoying immensely all of the commotion. I tired of it after a while and decided to go on to look for something else. Besides, most of the chickens had managed to hide themselves somewhere.

I travelled on down past the barn and found some calves feeding in a pen. I dashed in among them and barked and darted back and forth. They turned tail and headed for the far end of the pasture, bawling as they ran.

I had never had so much fun, and to be honest I felt quite heady with the new-found knowledge that I could put to rout anything on the Farm. I hadn't realized before that I had such power. All puffed up with my new importance, I went on looking.

Chapter 16

Pigs

Sept. 28, con't. — I came to a fenced in pen with a small building at one end. In front of the building, lying on her side in the warm fall sun, was a huge white pig. At her side, scattered along from front feet to hind feet were many little piglets all lined up in a neat row. The big pig lay perfectly still, now and then flicking an ear at an annoying fly that buzzed around her. The piglets wiggled and squirmed and occasionally squealed or grunted as they energetically set about the task of getting their dinner.

I eyed the strange looking family. The little ones were too absorbed in what they were doing to pay any attention to me, but the big one looked like a good possibility for fun. I wondered if she'd climb a tree like the cat if she were put to flight, or if she would scatter like the chickens, or run with her tail held high like the calves.

I pushed under the fence and approached her slowly, thinking just how much fun this was going to be. I walked carefully to within a few feet of her head and braced myself, hardly able to wait to see the pig's response.

When I got near her head I stopped. My she was big! Much bigger than the cat or the chickens. I took a deep breath and bounced on all four feet, barking loudly, anxious for all of the fun to commence. With one gigantic heave the big sow had thrust herself into the air and onto her feet. Little pigs came unplugged and flew in every direction, squealing and scampering as they hit the soft dirt.

With a grunt that fairly shook the ground on which I was standing, the pig tossed her head and came straight for me. I had expected her to run — but away from me not toward me. This new turn of events caught me off guard and I barely had time to turn tail and run yipping from the pen before the sow was upon me.

It was I who scrambled. I wished for a tree, but I knew instinctively that had one been there I wouldn't have been able to climb like the cat anyway.

The pig was very annoyed at having her sleep interrupted and in no way was she intimidated by a small dog.

I could feel her just behind me at every step and her grunting and snapping made me scurry even faster.

The little pigs were still running in circles, confused and upset about having their lunch time cut short, but I didn't even have time to enjoy the spectacle of their frustration. That big pig was close on my tail and I felt her weight shake that ground that I was attempting to cover as quickly as I could.

I had had no idea that it took such a long time to cover such a short distance, and I felt that I would be a goner long before I could reach the fence.

I finally reached the rails and with a quick duck I was under and out — not one second too soon, for as I scurried under the fence the sow hit me with her open jaws. Fortunately, before she was able to close them again I had tucked myself together just beyond her range, so all I got was a bruise from the knock of her hard jaw.

I was too frightened to even yip. My legs felt like jelly and my heart pounded. I didn't quit running until I reached the house, and then I crawled quickly under the porch and lay there panting for breath, still too scared to stir. That old pig continued circling her pen, grunting and snuffing and counting her piglets. I was afraid that she was still so mad that she might tear her way out of her pen and come looking for me.

Eventually she settled down and my heart returned to its normal pace. It was a long time until I felt brave enough to crawl out from under the porch again, and then it was only because Mark came looking for me to give me my lunch.

That afternoon I contented myself with staying close to the children, especially Mark, sharing in their games and following them to the creek.

As much as I would have enjoyed exploring the rest of the Farm, my experience with the big sow had unnerved me and I decided against it.

Just as my family was saying their last goodbys to the cousins and preparing to climb into the car for the return trip home, I sneaked away and dashed down to the pigpen. I approached it warily, and sure enough, there she was all stretched out again with that row of piglets neatly all plugged-in.

I crept as close to the fence as I dared and let out one wild bark. Again she wheeled upward scattering small pigs and grunting as she sprang.

I stayed only long enough to watch her angry head whirl around looking for me and those little pigs wiggling up from the dust and then I turned and ran for the safety of Mark and the car.

I rode home feeling pleased with myself. That old sow wasn't quite as big as she thought she was and I had licked her after all. My self-confidence was restored and I snuggled down on Mark's lap and prepared for sleep, grinning to myself.

The Farm sure is a fun place to be all right. No wonder Mark likes visiting there so much.

Chapter 17

Snow

Nov. 3 — Today when Grant came downstairs and looked out of the window he got all excited.

"It's snowing — it's snowing," he called.

The other children came running down and shrieked too.

"Look at the snow."

"See the snow."

"Can we play in it?"

Mrs. Dobson laughed and advised them to first get out of their pajamas and eat their breakfast.

They did, but as soon as breakfast was over they bundled up and were anxious to be off.

"Let's take Spunky."

"He's never seen snow."

Of course I had every intention of accompanying them. If *snow* caused that much excitement, I certainly wanted to see what it was all about.

I was carried outside. Overnight my backyard had changed completely. Over the lawn, the bushes, and the empty flower-beds there lay whiteness. I blinked. It had not been there before.

"What do you think of the snow, Spunky?"

So this was snow.

"Put him down — put him down and see what he does," cried Sandra.

Mark put me down. I expected to be able to run across the top of this white stuff, but to my surprise my feet sank right down in it. I took another step, attempting to stay up but again I sank. It was cold too. I lifted a paw and shook it, then another paw and shook it, but I couldn't get away from the white fluff or the cold.

I pushed my face into it. It was cold on my nose and it tickled. I sneezed — the light powder blew up around me. I sneezed again. The children were laughing.

"Let's make a snowman," Grant called and they all scrambled away to begin playing in the snow. I ran after them — or tried to. My short legs didn't work too well in the fluffy snow and I finally gave up running and lay down to roll, delighting in the feel of the softness.

Mark joined me and we rolled together. We scampered and tossed and kicked, making the snow fly all about us. Eventually we tired of our game and went to join the others with their snowman.

It was great fun in the snow; still, I was happy when it was time to go into the house. I was shivering some as I was placed in my box, and I lay there licking the ice particles out from between my toes. I was soon thawed out again and would have been glad to go out for another romp, but already the snow was disappearing from the yard. I felt disappointed about that. I guess Mark did too, for Mrs. Dobson comforted him by telling him that it was still too early for the snow to come and stay but there would be plenty more before the winter was over.

I sure hope that it comes again tomorrow.

Chapter 18

Tracy

Nov. 5 — Tracy was sick today so she didn't go to school. I was happy to have her stay home with me and was looking forward to having her to play with, but she really didn't feel much like playing. She did want me to stay with her though, so I lay quietly beside her until she fell asleep. I hope that she will soon be feeling better again. I like it better when she plays with me.

Nov. 8 — Tracy is still sick. Mrs. Dobson looked very worried this morning when she looked at the funny little thermometer that she took from Tracy's mouth. Then Mrs. Dobson called the doctor. He said that if Tracy weren't feeling better by the afternoon that he would come to see her. Mrs. Dobson phoned him again later and he came to the house. He left some medicine for Tracy.

Nov. 9 — We all try to be extra quiet. Mark took me up to see Tracy for awhile. She held me close. She felt very warm. I licked her face and she smiled but she didn't laugh.

Nov. 10 — Today they took Tracy away. Mark said that

she went to a hospital. Everybody is quiet and sad. Mark says that he hopes that Tracy is better soon so that she can come home again. He says at hospitals they make people feel better. I hope that they will make Tracy better real soon.

Nov. 11 — Tracy still isn't home and she still isn't better. Mrs. Dobson looks very worried and all of the children are still very quiet.

Nov. 13 — Today Mr. and Mrs. Dobson came home while the children were still at school. Mrs. Dobson cried and Mr. Dobson tried to comfort her but there were tears in his eyes too, then he went to the school and got Grant and Sandra and Mark.

Tracy is not going to come home again, Mark told me. He says that she went to a nice place called Heaven and that they will take good care of her there and that she will never be hurt or sick ever again. But Mark is sad. We all are sad. We miss Tracy very much.

Nov. 15 — Grant and Sandra and Mark are back at school today. I was lonely again when they all left this morning.

Mark held me close until the yellow school bus arrived. After the children left for school, Mrs. Dobson held me and loved me.

I think that she was lonesome too.

Nov. 17 — The children stayed home again today and went away with Mr. and Mrs. Dobson in the car. Grandpa and Grandma have been here for four days. The cousins came today but they didn't play much.

Nov. 18 — This is the weekend so we have two days without school. Grandpa and Grandma went home today. The cousins went back to the farm last night. Now we are all alone again.

Mark took me for a walk today. I saw Nero. We only said "Hello" to each other. We have been getting along much better lately but I didn't feel like talking.

Nov. 19 — The family went to Church today. I stayed home alone. I really didn't mind. Mrs. Dobson had a

long sleep this afternoon. We all tried to be very quiet.
Nov. 20 — The children are back in school. Mark said
that he'd "be seeing me" when he hurried out to the
yellow bus.

Chapter 19

Christmas

Dec. 18 — Today all of the children helped Mr. and Mrs. Dobson put up a Christmas tree. It looked like great fun but as they were working in the living room I had to watch from the door.

They stood a pine tree in a stand in front of the big window and then hung all sorts of shiny, pretty things all over it. It looked like magic — it glistened and glittered so. I would have loved to have played with some of the balls but I didn't want a paper-spank again.

After they were all finished they popped popcorn and we ate it together in the kitchen. Mark shared his with me.

Dec. 19 — We talked about Tracy today. Mr. Dobson said that he knew that we all loved and missed Tracy but that Tracy would want us to feel happy and to enjoy Christmas even though she won't be with us. Tracy is at a beautiful place — waiting to share it with us. Someday the whole family will be able to join her there. Mark said that he didn't want to go yet, even if he were missing Tracy, and Mrs. Dobson smiled and ruffled his hair.

"I'm glad that you're in no hurry," she said and her eyes looked misty.

I was glad too because I was afraid that Heaven might be like Church or School and I might have to wait at home.

Dec. 20 — While the children were at school today Mrs. Dobson wrapped presents in pretty paper and lots of ribbons and bows. She carried them in and put them under the tree. They all look so pretty there.

Christmas is getting closer.

Dec. 21 — Mrs. Dobson has been baking and baking. The whole house smells so good. When the children came home they got to "sample." Mark gave me a corner from his cookies. They taste as good as they smell.

Dec. 24 — Mrs. Dobson got out some big funny-looking stockings today. They had fancy things all over them. She said that they were Christmas stockings for the children to hang up. They each had a name on them. One of them said "Tracy," and Mrs. Dobson brushed away tears as she carefully placed it back in the box.

The children get to hang up their stockings tonight. I don't know why it is so special but they are excited about it.

Dec. 25 — Guess what! When we got up this morning all of those stockings were crammed full of super things.

Mark came squealing in first. He made so much racket that I decided to crawl out of bed and go see what was happening. He was busy pulling out toys and games, balloons and goodies.

Soon Sandra and Grant joined him and then Mr. and Mrs. Dobson came too, smiling even though they still looked sleepy.

You never saw such a commotion. I barked and yipped and wanted to join in. Mrs. Dobson pointed to a little stocking just for me and the children got excited all over again. There was a new collar — my old one was getting small — a new chewing-bone, some

special dog biscuits and a red ball. I acted as silly as the children.

Mark said that today Grandma and Grandpa and the cousins come, and today they unwrap all of the presents under the tree, and today they have Christmas dinner with turkey, and today they go to a special service at the Church where they sing and have the story of the Christ-child, and *all* of this because *today,* Christmas, is His birthday.

I knew that a dog couldn't do all of those things.

I did get presents and I did have fun with the cousins and I did get some of the special Christmas turkey and gravy for my dinner, but I didn't get to go to Church with the family. Even so, I enjoyed Christmas.

I hope that we will have another one — real soon. Dec. 26 — Mark informed me today that Christmas won't come again for a long, long time. I felt a little sad about that but then as he continued to talk to me, my spirits perked up again.

"You are getting 'big' Spunky. Well — not really big — but as big as you'll ever be. You are almost a grown-up dog now."

I felt kind of proud, being all grown up.

"I hope that you always like puppy games though Spunky 'cause I won't be grown-up for a *long* time yet. Dogs grow up a lot faster than boys do."

To assure Mark that I'd never be too "old" to play a lively game with my boy, I went for my new red ball and we soon had such a noisy game going that we were sent off to Mark's room to continue it there.

I thought about it more when I went to bed, tired out from our romp. Being grown-up was pretty special. It's a good thing that a dog gets to be grown-up and still can act like a puppy anytime that he wants.

Chapter 20

Goodby for Now

Well — guess that takes you through my puppy days. From then on my entries in my diary became a little more serious and subdued — though I definitely found out many times that I wasn't as grown-up as I tried to think. However, I did, over the months, manage to settle down some.

All in all I think that Mama would be proud of me. I have tried hard to uphold all of the rules that she instilled within me. She would have been happy too with the family that I care for. They are gentle, kind people and take good care of me — but that's enough. I'm sure that you are not one bit interested in the further reminiscing of an old dog. On the other hand, if you should be — perhaps you could drop in some day for a chat. There are many other adventures that I could share — if you would care to listen.